KU-502-637

Thorfinn
and the
Terrible Treasure

written by David MacPhail
illustrated by Richard Morgan

Young Kelpies

INDGAR VILLAGE, NORWAY

THORFINN'S
JOURNEY

TREASURE
ISLAND

CHAPTER 1

This story begins, as the best ones often do, with a mangy old elk standing on a hillside.

HA! Only kidding!

It starts, of course, with a treasure map...

Not with finding the map, which was, in itself, an interesting story...

Not even with the search for the treasure, a long and dangerous journey full of sword-fights and sea battles...

It begins with two fearsome Viking chiefs standing together on a sand dune in the remote Scottish Western Isles, watching their men dig a giant hole in the ground. On the treasure map, this is where 'X' marked the spot.

A spade struck solid wood, and everyone held their breath. But it was just someone's wooden leg.

" AAARGH!"

Luckily after a few more minutes digging, the spade struck wood again and this time the Vikings uncovered a solid-oak chest.

The two chiefs, who were from different villages around the same fjord in Norway, eyed each other like vultures.

"Remember our deal!" growled Harald the Skull-Splitter, Chief of Indgar village, and one of the most fearsome Viking warriors in the entire world.
His giant bushy beard glimmered gold in the sun.

"We split the loot equally," bellowed Magnus the Bone-Breaker, Chief of Vennagar village, which was right next door to Indgar.

"No tricks this time, Bone-Breaker!" Harald's eye twitched in the direction of his rival. Harald's eye always twitched when he was angry. Legend had it that even fully grown bears would run away when they saw his twitchy eye. "Any tricks, and we'll tie you to your ship's mast, sail you over the edge of the world and serve you up as supper to the krakens."

Magnus rolled his eyes and sighed. "Oh, don't be such a drama queen."

Harald's eye was now twitching so fast, it was practically popping out of his head. "I mean it!" he roared. "Or we'll make you walk the plank into a cess-pit!"

Down in the hole, the diggers clawed sand from around the chest and attached ropes to it.

"HEEEAVE!"

The men at the top of the hole hauled it into the air and threw it onto the sand at the feet of the chiefs.

"Get me something to break the lock!" boomed Harald.

A large man grabbed the nearest solid object to hand, which happened to be a wooden leg.

"Aaargh! Gimme a break!" cried the one-legged Viking, who had been trying to put it back on.

Harald gave the leg a mighty swing... and
smashed the lock into pieces, and the leg too.

Holding their breath, the two chiefs prised open
the lid of the chest, and threw it back.

CHAPTER 2

The Vikings' wildest dreams had come true.

The chest was overflowing with treasure.

"I'm rich! I'll never have to pillage again!"

Magnus grabbed a handful of precious stones.

"Knock it off!" cried Harald, snatching the stones away. "No one touches the loot until we've counted it."

The two chiefs snarled at each other, with fists clenched white around the hilts of their swords. Their men did likewise.

A small boy who had a pigeon perched on his shoulder finally broke the stand-off. "Pardon me," he said, raising his helmet. "But shall we have a spot of supper? Nobody can enjoy their work on an empty stomach." He knelt down to speak to the one-legged Viking. "And I'll gladly make you a new leg, old pal." This was Thorfinn, Harald's son – a very unusual Viking. Unusual because he was *nice*. VERY nice. In fact, his Viking name was Thorfinn the Very-Very-Nice-Indeed. Being nice was *not* something Vikings were known for.

"By ODIN'S BEARD!" cried Harald. "Yes, Thorfinn my boy! But we can do much better than a spot of supper. We'll have a feast, A FEAST! Let there be food! And ale! And burping!"

BAAAARP!

"YESSS!" cried Magnus, forgetting his differences with Harald, and joining in with a rip-roaring belch:

BUUUURRRRP!

They all headed down to the beach to prepare the fire and begin the festivities.

"WAIT!" said Harald. "We need someone to guard the treasure. Just in case."

The two chiefs once more ogled each other suspiciously. Their hands once again reached for their sword hilts. "GRRRR!"

"My men will guard it," said Magnus.

Harald burst into laughter. "HA! *Your* men?"

"What?" shrugged Magnus, pretending to be offended. "Don't you trust me?"

"I wouldn't trust your men to guard a pot of reindeer stew," said Harald. "No, I'll put my best man on it. I'll take personal responsibility."

Magnus rubbed his beard. "What did you say?

You'll take personal responsibility?"

"Yes, my guard is so trustworthy, I'd stake my entire village on him." Harald puffed out his chest.

"There... *you* heard him," Magnus whispered to his crew. "If anything goes missing it's on him, and we get his village too."

Harald's second-in-command, Erik the

Ear-Masher, nudged Harald on the elbow. Erik only had one eye. The other was covered by an eye patch. His face was like a squashed cabbage and his black beard was almost as large and bushy as Harald's. "Watch it, Chief! That piece of elk dung called Magnus has been trying to steal Indgar village from us for years."

Harald hesitated, but he couldn't back down now without losing face. "Nothing will go missing under my man's nose."

"It's a deal then," said Magnus. "But tell me, what kind of fearsome shield-warrior, what kind of savage wolf-wrestler do you have for a guard, that you would stake your entire village on him?"

Harald turned and bellowed,

"THORFINN!"

Thorfinn was collecting driftwood for the fire.

He turned and raised his helmet once again.

"Yes, my dear sirs, how can I be of assistance?"

CHAPTER 3

Erik the Ear-Masher stared at Harald in wide-eyed horror. "Thorfinn?! Thorfinn is going to guard all that lovely treasure?!"

Magnus burst out in deep, booming laughter. "THIS is your savage wolf-wrestler?! He'd have trouble wrestling a kitten."

Harald shrugged. "He may not look much of a Viking, but he's smart, he's proved himself many times in the past, and he's the most honest of us all."

Beside Thorfinn were his two best friends. Velda was a tiny girl with red hair and an oversized helmet.

She glared at the chiefs, swinging her axe about, as if ready to crack someone on the head at the slightest excuse. "Wotcha!" she said gruffly.

Then there was Oswald, the wise man of Indgar village, who was incredibly old and had an incredibly long beard. He'd perfected the art of sleeping on his feet, and was snoozing gently, his head lolled to one side.

"Hey, is that old man actually asleep?" asked Magnus.

Oswald let loose a loud, ripping snore.

"ZZZZZZZZ!"

Harald knelt down and placed a mighty arm around his son's shoulders. "Now, Thorfinn, guard the treasure with your life. The fate of Indgar rests in your hands. I know you won't let me down. I'll send someone up to the dunes with your food."

"Why, of course, dear Father. I'll do anything to help," replied Thorfinn.

"Good lad!" Harald went off towards the beach, rubbing his hands and whistling. "Oh, goodie! A feast! I'm starving!"

Erik shouted after him, "You can't stake the whole village on Thorfinn! How will he defend himself if someone attacks him? By throwing scones at them? We need another guard." He turned and bellowed in the direction of his

own son, who was down on the beach digging a
pit for the fire.

"O-LAAAFFFF!"

Olaf was a large boy who took after his father
in the looks department. He also had a face like
a cabbage, one that had gone mouldy and been
trampled by a herd of elks.

"Why me?!" he huffed as he reached them. "Why do you always pick me? People are going to think me and Thorfinn are friends."

"I'd be more worried about that if I was Thorfinn," scoffed Velda.

"Oh, ha ha!" said Olaf scowling.

"I'll help you guard the treasure, Thorfinn – no thieves will get past me." Velda flashed her axe.

"Thank you so much for your kind offer," said Thorfinn, "but I wouldn't dream of troubling you. Go and enjoy the feast."

CHAPTER 4

Viking feasts were a long, messy, riotous business. They often lasted several days, after which the 'survivors' couldn't remember why they'd started feasting in the first place.

While the meal was being cooked, Harald declared a wrestling contest, which he promptly won. He took on three men at once, lifting each of them up over his head, spinning them round and launching them into the crowd.

"YAHHHH!"

Some of the spectators took exception to having other Vikings thrown at them. They snarled and leapt into the ring to join the fight.

Another group of men launched into a Viking

song:

"Oh, oh, oh, oh, Vikings will a-hunting go,
Ay, ay, ay ay, hunting all the live-long day."

Harald gazed across the beach full of Vikings, singing, making merry and throwing punches at one another, and he laughed – a gigantic bellowing laugh that erupted from his great barrel-shaped chest. "OHHHH, I do love a good feast!"

Soon the food was put down in front of them and the men set upon it like snapping crocodiles. They ripped apart meat with their bare hands, gnawing on bones and spitting out gristly bits for their dogs to fight over.

Afterwards, Magnus the Bone-Breaker climbed on top of a barrel.

"VIKINGS!" His booming voice brought about an unusual moment of quiet. "I have exactly sixty-five men in my crew. As a special treat, you're about to see each and every one of them walk over hot coals."

The watching crowd looked puzzled. Sure enough, Magnus's men were all lined up, barefoot, in front of the fire. They looked far from eager.

Magnus stood at the other side of the fire pit and urged them forward. "Hurry up, you cretins! Move it!"

Velda watched, unimpressed, as the men tiptoed across, yelping in pain. "What exactly is the point of this?" She turned to Oswald, who'd fallen asleep again. "I'm off to take Thorfinn and Olaf some food, OK?"

Oswald let loose another rasping snore.

"I'll take that as a yes," she muttered, rolling her eyes.

She collected a tray and two bowls, and dolloped steaming-hot spoonfuls of stew into them, before filling up two mugs of water from a barrel. As she was making her way through the crowd, a tall, cloaked figure barged into her and nearly knocked the food flying.

"Oi!" she screamed after him, shaking her fist. "You wanna watch it, mate!"

She caught a flash of ginger hair from under the hood, and a braided beard. But the figure ducked out of sight. "Tchoh! Some people!" She shook her head and climbed the slope into the dunes, where she found Thorfinn and Olaf guarding the treasure, warming their hands by a small fire.

"Hello, Thorfinn, here's your dinner." She held out the tray towards him.

"Why thank you, old pal," replied Thorfinn, taking his bowl.

"Oh, and I brought yours too, turnip features." She plonked Olaf's bowl down on the sand.

Velda sat with them while they ate. The sun was beginning to set over the sea.

"I can stay up here if you like?" said Velda.

"I wouldn't dream of inconveniencing you," said Thorfinn. "The festivities will last all night – go and enjoy yourself. Olaf and I will take turns to keep watch."

"OK." Velda got up, wiping the sand off her hands. "There's an axe-throwing competition in a while and I'm going to win it! See you in the morning."

Olaf watched her go then yawned. "Oh, I'm tired.

I might just doze off. You take the first watch, Thorfinn."

"Right you are, old bean," said Thorfinn.

Olaf rolled over and fell fast asleep. But soon, Thorfinn began to feel sleepy too. It was a strange, heavy sort of sleepiness that he'd never felt before. He shook his head.

"Percy, I mustn't go to sleep," he whispered urgently to his pet pigeon. "I must stay awake and guard the treasure."

Percy gave him a gentle peck on the nose, followed by a sharp one.

But, try as he might, Thorfinn couldn't keep his eyes open. The next thing he knew he was dreaming about hurtling downhill in a cart, being tossed from side to side.

Thorfinn woke with a huge jolt.

It was daylight.

Someone was shaking him and lots of angry Viking faces were glaring down at him.

"Thorfinn! THORFINN!" It was his father, shaking him furiously. "Thorfinn, where's the treasure?"

"Hmm?"

There was a large hollow in the sand where the chest had stood. The treasure had gone.

CHAPTER 5

"Where's our treasure, boy?!" growled Erik the Ear-Masher.

"Oh dear," replied Thorfinn. "I really don't know. Olaf and I were..."

"ASLEEP!" cried Harald. "You were snoring, counting elks, while someone made off with our loot!"

Percy, who was perched on a log nearby, shrugged and seemed to scratch his head with his wing.

Erik the Ear-Masher was dangling his son Olaf by the scruff of the neck. "I think someone put something in our food!" Olaf croaked.

"Yes! Of course!" said Harald. He glowered at Magnus, who was standing back, his arms folded and a smug expression on his face. "I knew it, Bone-Breaker! This is your trickery."

"*Me?!*" Magnus looked insulted, in an over-the-top sort of way. "You accuse *me*?"

"You wanted all the treasure for yourself, you rat!"

"That's ridiculous," Magnus replied. "How could *I* have done it? Me and my men were on the beach. You counted each and every one of them, walking over hot coals."

There was no denying it. "He's right. It couldn't have been him," Harald said in a daze.

"You know what this means, don't you, Chief?" growled Erik.

"Oh yes," said Magnus, with an even-smugger-if-that-was-possible look. "Harald gave us his personal guarantee, which means..."

Harald's face was white. "I lose my village. I've lost Indgar."

There was a moment's stunned silence as Harald's men took this in.

"Exactly," said Magnus, laughing. "But there's good news too. It means I've gained a village!"

Suddenly there was a loud cry, which sounded a bit like a seagull throwing up.

"HOOOOLLLLLD ON!"

It was Oswald.

"You can't have our village yet, and I'll tell you why—" Before he could say anything further he tripped over his beard and fell flat on his face.

Thorfinn helped him up.

Oswald dusted himself off and continued. "Viking law is clear. Our chief has fourteen days to either find the treasure or pay back its value. If he can't complete his task, *then* you can have the village.

"OOF!"

They don't call me the wise man for nothing,"
he added.

Erik snorted, kicking up dust with his boot.
"Whoever made off with the chest is long gone.
We'll never find the treasure again."

Magnus agreed. "And as for paying us back, there
was a fortune in that chest. You'll never be able to
raise enough money."

Harald growled. "Well, we're going to try!"

Magnus shrugged. "Oh, well, fine. Fourteen days it is.
Also," he added, "you have to leave your two guards
behind on the island until the time is up." He
leaned into Thorfinn and Olaf's faces and sneered.
"Marooned and alone..."

"What for?" Harald protested.

"Punishment!"

"They're just boys!"

"You should have thought of that before you put them in charge of the loot, you oaf!"

Harald swallowed the insult, and Magnus led his men back to their longships and set sail. Erik stomped off in a huff and kicked a boulder.

"OWWWW!"

"What do we do now, Chief?" asked Harald's men.

"We'll head back to Indgar," said Harald. "We'll have to find a way of raising the money."

The Indgar Vikings turned towards their ships – all except Velda. "I'm staying," she said.

Thorfinn's face lit up. "Are you really, old friend?

Oh, it'll be such fun. We can have campfires and sing-songs and tell stories."

"Aargh! Throw me in the sea!" cried Olaf. "Anything's better than fourteen days stuck in this hell-hole with you two."

"Belt up, spud-face!" snapped Velda.

"Well, *I'm* not staying!" said Oswald, sounding like an annoyed gannet as he turned away. "The sand plays havoc with my bunions."

Harald loitered behind his men, reluctant to leave his son. Thorfinn tugged gently at his father's bearskin cape. "Dearest Dad, why don't you let me take the *Green Dragon*? We'll go searching for the treasure. I'm sure we can get to the bottom of all this."

The *Green Dragon* was Thorfinn's own longship,

which Harald had recently gifted to his son. Harald stroked his giant bushy beard. "Hmmm... Magnus said you were to stay here until the fourteen days are up."

"So?" said Velda. "How will they know?"

"So..." He hesitated for a moment. "I can't allow it. The *Green Dragon* comes home with me."

Velda groaned with disappointment. Thorfinn gave a light-hearted shrug. "OK, my dear old dad." He reached up and hugged his father.

"Farewell, son." Harald's eyes were moist as he turned briskly for the ship.

"Farewell, Father," cried Thorfinn, as Indgar's longships pushed off without them. "I hope to see you again soon."

The three children gazed out across their new home, which was sad and treeless and populated only by a few mangy goats.

CHAPTER 6

Thorfinn, Velda and Olaf climbed to the island's highest point, a rocky windswept crag, and watched the ships sail off. Percy flitted high above them.

Through his spyglass, which he always carried, Thorfinn could see his dad at the stern of his longship, staring back sadly in their direction.

Thorfinn waved enthusiastically. "COO-EEE, Father!"

Olaf tutted. "What have you got to COO-EEE about? Look at this dump."

"Oh, quit moaning, potato features," said Velda.

Thorfinn swung his spyglass round in the other direction and pointed it at a distant speck on the horizon. It was a ship, and it was sailing southwards, away from the island. "Hmm, that's strange."

"What's strange?"

Thorfinn handed Olaf the spyglass. "Pardon me, but do you see that ship?"

"Yes," said Olaf, "but what's so strange about it?"

"Don't you notice anything unusual?"

Olaf took another long look. "Single mast, square sail, double-ended, forty oars. So what?"

Velda sighed. "Gimme."
She snatched the spyglass
off Olaf and squinted

48

through it. "It's one of those big Scottish galleys. And forty oars means it's someone fancy. You don't see many of those about." She handed the spyglass back to Thorfinn.

"Oh, very well done, my dear pal." He grinned, and patted Velda on the shoulder. "Anyone with forty oars is important, possibly even royalty, and the ship is hot-footing it away from this island."

Olaf's eyes lit up. "You think it could be the treasure thieves?"

"Perhaps..." Thorfinn scratched his cheek for a moment, deep in thought, before waving his finger. "Aha! Follow me!"

He turned away, before turning back again and adding, "That is, if you wouldn't mind."

"Oh, get on with it!" Velda shoved him forwards.

Thorfinn led them back down to the spot where the treasure had been stolen. He paced around for a moment, his arms clasped behind his back, peering down at the ground.

"What are you searching for?" Velda asked. "You look like a bird strutting about on the sand."

"That!" Thorfinn pointed out a long trail of raked sand heading south. "The thieves brushed over their footprints with branches to hide their tracks. Very clever, except that it leaves a trail of brush marks instead. Come on!"

He dashed off, before dashing back and adding, "That is, if it's not too inconvenient."

"Oh, move it!" yelled Velda.

Thorfinn led them to a beach on the south side of the island, where he stopped.

"This is where the treasure was loaded." He pointed at some marks in the sand. "The brush marks divide near the water, which suggests a number of small boats beached here. They were probably serving a bigger boat that was anchored offshore."

"That big galley!" Olaf strutted around, his face flushing red, then punched his palm with his fist. "We have to go after them. We have to track them down and get back our treasure."

51

"Brilliant idea, birdbrain," said Velda. "Except we're stuck here."

Just then, the prow of a longship appeared around the sea cliffs, topped with a green dragon head.

CHAPTER 7

"It's the *Green Dragon*!" cried Olaf.

Thorfinn's devoted crew waved to their friends on the beach and cheered. The ship beached nearby.

First to greet Thorfinn was Harek the Toe-Stamper, who was the chief warrior on board. He was a big man with wild eyes, although that might have been because they were both pointing in different directions. He was also the most accident-prone man in Norway.

"Thorfinn, Hell-OHHHH!" Harek swung off the side of ship from a rope, only to realise he'd forgotten to tie the other end to anything. He hit the ground like a sack of spuds.

BOOOOF!

Next they saw Grimm the Grim, the helmsman: a sad-faced man who was always miserable. Even his beard seemed droopy.

"I don't suppose Thorfinn even remembers who I am," he moaned in his long, droning voice. "I wouldn't if I were him."

The ship's cook was Gertrude the Grotty, a warty-faced, greasy-haired woman whose chief speciality was recipes with insects: in particular, flies, several of which were constantly orbiting her head.

She banged her pot with a spoon and shrieked, "Thorfinn, I've gots a nice bowl of lentil and cockroach soup here for you!"

Then there was Grut the Goat-Gobbler, a short, tubby man, whose stomach was always grumbling. He was eyeing the livestock roaming the island.

"Mmmm, those wild goats look tasty."

A tall, golden-haired man swung over the side of the *Green Dragon*, landed on the beach beside Thorfinn and grinned. It was Torsten the Ship-Sinker, Thorfinn's navigator. His Viking name sounded impressive, until it became clear that the only ships he'd ever sunk were his own. Unfortunately, he was not very good with directions.

"I knew we'd find you here," he told Thorfinn. "Oswald said you'd be at the south of the island, but I knew it would be the north."

"But, my dear friend, this *is* the south of the island," replied Thorfinn.

"Oh," said Torsten, scratching his head.

Oswald was there too, craning his head over the side, waving his walking stick and yelling in his loud, whiny voice, "Come aboard immediately, you young fool!"

While Torsten prised Harek out of the sand, Thorfinn climbed the rope, with Velda close behind.

"Aren't you coming, old pal?" Thorfinn called back to Olaf.

Olaf gazed around at the island, as if weighing up his options. Then he sighed and grabbed the rope. "I can't believe I'm going to sea with these losers AGAIN."

Thorfinn vaulted the ship's rail and embraced his crew. "Thank you so much, everyone. But how did you manage to get away from the others?"

"Chief Harald sent us back to help you," said Torsten. "He wanted the others to think we'd left you behind, then he told us to skip away when they entered a fog bank."

"He thinks Magnus stole the treasure," said Harek. "Up to his old tricks as usual."

"Your father believes you are the only one who can solve this mystery *and* save the village," said Oswald.

Then Olaf cut in, telling the others about the forty-oared galley they'd seen heading south. "It'll be way out of sight now, though, and it's much too fast for us."

"What shall we do, Thorfinn?" asked Velda.

"Ahem…" Thorfinn cleared his throat, smiled and stepped onto a barrel to address the crew. "My dear friends, there's no denying it: this will be our most challenging adventure yet."

"Why?" said Grut. "Have we run out of food?"

"Well, I'm up for anything," said Torsten, "as long as it doesn't involve going further south."

"We're going south," announced Thorfinn.

"Oh," said Torsten.

"Wait! I've got another idea to get our money

back!" shouted Olaf. "Instead of trying to chase that treasure, let's do what we Vikings do best – pillage! In fact, we could raid every town between here and Norway."

This brought a murmur of approval, until Thorfinn swiped his hands through the air, sending Percy fluttering around his shoulders.

"My dear friends," said Thorfinn. "There will be no pillaging. We're going to search for that galley and track down the treasure that's rightfully ours. They probably plan to stop at the nearest port heading south – Dunadd City."

CHAPTER 8

On the third morning of their voyage south, Thorfinn and his crew woke to a cold fog and the sound of Grut shamelessly wolfing down the last of their supplies.

"Nom, nom . . . *schlom, schlom . . . "*

They threaded their way through a gap between two craggy islets, and into a large natural harbour. A smoky, ramshackle town spread out along the shoreline.

"Dunadd City," muttered Oswald, who was standing at Thorfinn's shoulder. "The capital of the Scots. A wretched place, full of cutpurses, bootleggers and gamblers." The narrow, tightly packed buildings rose up to a wooden hill fort perched on a rock. "And the worst of them lives in that castle – the rogue King Appin," Oswald continued.

They tied up at the pier, checking all the boats in the harbour. There was no sign of the huge galley they'd seen speeding away from the treasure island.

"Let's ask around," said Thorfinn. He picked out a warty, toothless old fisherman hobbling along in front of them. "Ah, this looks like a fine fellow."

Velda snorted. She'd seen finer fellows dug up from a grave.

Thorfinn raised his helmet to the man. "Good day, my dear sir. Would you happen to have seen a forty-oared galley docking here?"

The man gulped down his surprise, as he was not expecting such politeness from a Viking. "Aye, there's only the one in these waters. That's the king's boat, the *Sea Viper*."

"I see," replied Thorfinn, sharing a look with Oswald and Velda. "And have you seen this boat around recently?"

"The king himself waved her off four days ago and she has not yet returned."

The fisherman hobbled off, and Velda punched a wall. "That *has* to be it!"

"We could head back out to sea and look for it?" said Torsten.

"Yes!" said Olaf. "We could find her, board her and fight the crew."

"No," yawned Oswald. "I'm too tired for all that rubbish. I need a nap." And he let his head fall to one side.

"ZZZZZ..."

"There's no time to lose, Thorfinn! We have to find that treasure or Indgar will be lost!" cried Velda.

"Hmmm..." Thorfinn sat down on the pier and drummed his fingers on his chin. Percy perched beside him and fluttered his wing. "Even if the king's ship isn't here right now, the chances are it will return at some point because the king is here."

"Thorfinn's right," said Harek.

"So," said Thorfinn, "if we want to find the ship, the best thing we can do is to wait."

"What do you mean, 'wait'?" asked Olaf. "We're Vikings! We don't WAIT!"

The silence was only broken by Grut's stomach rumbling.

"That reminds me," said Velda, "we've run out of food! We don't even have a biscuit left. Grut's eaten it all."

"Yes, and I'm still starving," Grut complained.

"And, more importantly, we don't have any money left to buy anything," added Velda.

Gertrude nodded. "There's is some lovely

harbour midgies, I've noticed. I could make yous a nice midgie and weevil hotpot."

Velda made a sick face. "I'd rather eat my shoe."

"There's nothing else for it," said Thorfinn, getting to his feet. "We'll have to get jobs."

The crew groaned. "WHAT??!"

"HOOLLLLD your horses!" said Olaf. "Vikings don't do jobs. I'm NOT getting a job."

"Cork it, pumpkin features," said Velda, twirling her axe at him. "Or maybe you'd rather starve?"

"Well, quite, and remember: if we don't find that galley, getting jobs and saving our money will be the only way of paying back the other chiefs for the stolen treasure," said Thorfinn.

"That's rubbish," said Olaf. "We're Vikings!

Can't we just nick it?"

"Oh, dear, no," said Thorfinn, horrified. "We have to obtain the money honestly."

They looked around them. The harbour was a colourful, bustling place, with dock workers hauling goods on and off ships, hawkers selling their wares, and gangs of pickpockets eyeing the chance to steal from unsuspecting sailors.

Fortunately for Thorfinn's crew, Velda swinging

her axe about was enough to scare them all off. That, and the smell of Gertrude.

"Look," said Harek, pointing at a dusty sign on a wall nearby. It looked like it had been there for decades.

CHAPTER 9

Meanwhile, back in Norway...

Thorfinn's home village of Indgar was nestled beside a beautiful fjord. It was a tranquil place, except for the folk who lived there, who spent their days roaring, skirmishing, farting, burping and brawling, not to mention a great deal of HUZZAH-ing.

But today was different.

Very different.

The Vikings were anything but their usual selves.

They assembled in the square and listened to their chief delivering the bad news.

"We have ten days left, either to find the missing treasure or pay back Magnus," Harald the Skull-Splitter said sadly. "Or he will take over the village."

He looked round at their shocked faces, and his heart sank. *This is all my fault,* he thought. *I've let them down. Even worse, I've let my own son down too. My little boy.*

He wondered where Thorfinn was now, and whether the crew he had sent in the *Green Dragon* had rescued him. He would never forgive himself if something bad happened to Thorfinn.

Erik the Ear-Masher roared with frustration, hoisted a barrel over his head, and launched it into the air. It flew across the square and crashed through the cowshed wall.

"Enough of feeling sorry for ourselves!" he cried.
Then he climbed onto a mound of turnips, which
the Vikings never ate, of course, as turnips are
vegetables. They used them either as elk feed or as
ammunition for their catapults. Erik poked a finger
at his chief. "Harald's to blame. He led us to this."

The other Vikings gasped. Erik was challenging
the chief himself.

Harald's eye twitched at Erik. "I'll have no more
of your insolence, Ear-Masher!" He whipped out his
sword and leapt at his second-in-command.

Erik drew his own sword. Sparks flew – not to
mention bits of turnip – as the
two men clashed in the square.
They locked swords,
face to face.

"You one-eyed
snake!" growled
Harald.

"You two-eyed
weasel!" snarled Erik.

A terrifying scream
pierced the air like

a blade, and a figure jumped between them and pulled them off one another.

It was Thorfinn's mother, Freya, her fierce green eyes staring out from under a mane of blonde hair. She grabbed the two men by the ears. "Our village is under threat, and you two are fighting each other?"

Grown men were known to weaken at the knees under Freya's steely glare, and these two were no different – even Harald, a man who was known as 'The Terror of the North Sea'."

"Sorry, dear," he said sheepishly.

She tugged Erik's ear. "You say sorry too!"

"Ow! OK! Sorry," said Erik, and she let them go.

Freya pushed the two men away and stood alone on top of the mound of turnips, staring round at the villagers' faces.

"Everyone!" she yelled. "Dig up what valuables you have and bring them here to the marketplace. Let's see if we can pay off some of this debt."

The villagers turned away. Harald reddened under his wife's savage gaze. He wondered if she would ever forgive him for bargaining away their village and putting their son at risk – or if he could ever forgive himself.

CHAPTER 10

Back in the Scots' capital of Dunadd, Thorfinn and his crew stared at the VIKING JOB CENTRE sign.

"Ah-ha!" said Thorfinn. "That's just the ticket."

The sign led them along an alleyway, then up a rickety flight of steps, until they came to a tiny, bare office lit only by a small window. A scruffy old man wearing fingerless gloves was sitting behind a dusty desk. He looked surprised to see them.

"Can I help you?" he asked.

Thorfinn approached the desk while the rest of the crew squeezed in behind him. He removed his helmet and beamed. "Good day, my dear sir. We're Vikings and we're looking for jobs."

"Are you? Really?" The man's face lit up and he punched the air. "Oh, that's WONDERFUL! I haven't had a single customer since I opened."

"When did you open?" asked Olaf.

"Thirty years ago." The man grabbed Thorfinn's hand and shook it up and down. "So you must forgive my excitement. My name's Wibblish."

The Vikings sniggered, apart from Thorfinn, who was much too polite to laugh at people's names.

Mr Wibblish was so enthusiastic he didn't even notice.

"You see, everyone is scared of the Vikings," he explained, "but I've always thought, if I could give Vikings a more positive purpose in life – other than raiding and pillaging – they'd be less scary. I've made this my life's mission."

"What a clown!" declared Olaf loudly.

Velda jabbed him in the ribs with her elbow. "Sssh!"

"People have laughed at me for years. I was almost on the point of giving up, but now you're here!" said Mr Wibblish. He rubbed his hands together with glee. "Oh, this is so exciting! Now, first thing's first... Let's see...

But of course!"

He pulled some parchment forms from a drawer, picked up a piece of charcoal and rolled his sleeves up. "I'll interview you one at a time. You first, miss."

He waggled his finger at Gertrude, who fluttered her eyelashes, which unfortunately disturbed the fly that was sitting there.

"Me? Miss?" She giggled and blushed. "Tee hee!"

"First name?" he asked.

"Gertrude!" she shrieked.

"Surname?"

"They calls me 'The Grotty'. I don'st know why."

"Date of birth?"

"Oh, I'm not sure, but I am only twenty-five, as you can see from my bea-oo-tiful skin."

"Place of birth?" he asked.

"The cowshed," said Gertrude.

"I was born there, too," said Grimm. "And people wonder why I'm miserable."

"Do you have any qualifications?" asked Mr Wibblish.

Gertrude stroked one of her favourite warts before replying, "Hmmm... I can wrestle giant dung beetles, threes at a time. POP! Into the soup they go."

81

"And do you have any work experience?"

"I cooks, sir."

The Vikings burst out laughing, but Mr Wibblish didn't notice. "Oh, that's wonderful," he said. "Good cooks are always in demand round here."

The word 'good' caused another outburst of laughter.

"OK – next!" said Mr Wibblish, putting Gertrude's form to one side.

Grut was the next to take a seat at Mr Wibblish's desk.

"And you? What's your date of birth?"

"Not sure," replied Grut. "Though it was during the Spring Festival, a feast that lasted twelve whole days." His eyes took on a dreamy, faraway look.

"Elk, oxen, horse meat, beef... mmm... all washed down with a vat of mead. That was my first meal."

Harek raised his hand. "I was born during the

Great Eclipse – the year of the devastating volcano. The harvests all failed and the trees turned black."

"Why does that not surprise me?" muttered Velda.

Then it was Torsten's turn. "What's your occupation?" asked Mr Wibblish.

"Navigator," replied Torsten proudly.

"Oh, that's wonderful, and which ships have you worked on?"

Torsten began to count them off: "The *Death Bucket*, The *Fish Fodder*, The *Jinx*, The *Jonah*, The *Mild Sense of Doom*..."

Mr Wibblish scratched his head with a bit of charcoal. "Never heard of any of them."

"I'm not surprised," said Velda. "They're all at the bottom of the sea."

When it was his turn, Olaf puffed out his cheeks. "Do we have to go through this rubbish? No wonder Vikings don't work. This is ridiculous!"

Once Mr Wibblish had completed a form for each of them, he turned to a drawer marked 'VACANCIES' and slowly thumbed through a pile of parchment. By this time the Vikings were climbing the walls with boredom. They couldn't even get their swords out and practise fighting, as there wasn't enough room in the office to move their elbows.

"Ah-ha!" Mr Wibblish said eventually. "It seems you're in luck. There's a big feast tonight at the castle. King Appin is entertaining the French Ambassador. They're in desperate need of extra staff!"

CHAPTER 11

In his chamber in Dunadd Castle, King Appin admired himself in the mirror. His tartan robes were made from the finest cloth imported from Paris and Milan. He looked down at his bare feet and sighed with annoyance.

"Where's that man I sent tae the cobblers?" he barked at his attendants, who all looked either confused or terrified or both. Only the smallest servant offered an explanation. He was wearing a quartered tunic, as was the pigeon perched on his shoulder.

"Excuse me, my dear sir," Thorfinn said with a rosy-cheeked smile.

"How DARE you talk to me?" King Appin exploded. "You're a wee pageboy. You don't talk. Dae ye understand?"

Thorfinn smiled and bowed, before stepping back and doffing his helmet. "Pardon me, your majesty. I was just going to say that my good friend Torsten is a wonderful man, but perhaps not the best choice of person to navigate the streets of Dunadd, or indeed anywhere."

The king kicked up his bare feet. "Och! What am I supposed to wear on my feet? This feast is already a complete disaster and our guests haven't even arrived yet." He clicked his fingers and led the troupe of men, including Thorfinn, into the great hall.

A table ran the entire length of the hall, and had been piled high with mountains of food. King Appin clearly liked to impress important people with big feasts.

There was one problem, though. Several of the platters were already empty.

The king stopped in his tracks. All that remained of his favourite dish, skewered partridge, were a few pathetic bones.

Grut the Goat-Gobbler was working his way up the table, demolishing platters one by one. And Grut was a messy eater: he scattered bits of food all over the floor and all over his tunic as he went.

"Hey YOU!" cried the king. "Just whit dae ye think you're doing?"

Grut waited until he'd swallowed the whole chicken he was devouring before replying, "I'm your new food taster."

"You're supposed to be just *tasting* it, ye muckle great loon!"

Grut shrugged. "Can I help it if I swallow some?"

Thorfinn stepped forward again and bowed. "Ahem... your majesty..." He paused, before continuing, "My friend Grut is a cheerful and brave fellow, but he's possibly the worst man in the world to put in charge of a feast, or even, for that matter, a plate of biscuits."

"Wait a minute," said the king, running his finger over the tabletop. "The table is filthy! Why hasn't the room been cleaned?"

One of his attendants coughed. "The housekeeping staff all went home, Sire. They said they were depressed."

91

Thorfinn interrupted yet again. "Excuse me, your highness..."

"WHAT? Why do you keep talking, wee boy?!" snarled the king.

"I was just about to suggest that my friend Grimm the Grim, while being a stout fellow of some ability, is perhaps not the kind of sparkling team player your already hard-pressed housekeeping staff needed."

King Appin started to speak, but then he stopped abruptly, sniffed, opened the lid of a pot, picked up a ladle and sampled the dark brown stew inside. "EUCH!" He spat it out. "Whit's this? It's disgusting!"

"Midgie and dung-beetle stew," said Thorfinn. "Freshly made by your new chef, Gertrude."

The king turned green with horror and hurled

the pot towards Thorfinn, who leapt nimbly out of the way.

"KINGS DO NOT EAT MIDGIIEEES!!!"

Just then horns sounded to announce the arrival of the French Ambassador.

CHAPTER 12

A door opened in the side wall of King Appin's great hall, and in walked the French Ambassador: a tall, noble-looking man wearing exquisite clothes. Unfortunately, his appearance was somewhat ruined by the fact that he smelt very strongly of rotten cabbage.

An attendant leaned over to whisper into Thorfinn's ear, "You'll get used to the smell. The drains in French palaces are terrible."

"Welcome, Lord Camembert," said the king, and the two men embraced each other warmly.

Camembert began to speak in French.

"Oh, crivvens," said the king. "Where's my translator?"

Oswald appeared at the king's shoulder. "*Oui?*"

King Appin coughed a little, then held a silk scarf up to his nose to mask the ambassador's awful smell. "Oof, whit a stench! Tell Lord Camembert how pleased I am that he's here."

Oswald nodded, turned to the Frenchman and spoke a few words, at which Camembert's face turned red and he began to bellow angrily.

"Whit did ye say to him, ye great numptie?"

the king demanded of Oswald.

"What you told me to say," Oswald replied.
"That he smells and that you're pleased to see him."

"WHITTT!?" Now it was the king's turn to go red.
"You told the French Ambassador he stinks? Ye great
eejit! Tell him I'm sorry – right this minute!"

Oswald turned back to Lord Camembert and said
something else. This time the Frenchman reacted
even more angrily and gripped his sword.

"What did you say to him this time?"

"I told him you're sorry that he stinks." Oswald
shrugged. "I thought that's what you wanted."

"You fool! You've embarrassed my guest!"

"He should be embarrassed," said Oswald.
"That smell is *revolting.*"

"Get oot ma sight!" yelled the king. "You're the worst translator ever!"

Oswald shrugged and walked out.

Before the king could do anything to calm his guest down there was a colossal crash from the fireplace, and the whole hall was engulfed in soot.

"AAARGH!" he yelled, coughing. "Whit now?"

Black dust settled over everything, including their fine clothes, the king's bare feet and all the food. Something small and Viking-shaped climbed out of the fireplace, wafting away the soot. It was Velda.

"Wotcha! I'm your new chimney sweep."

There was another colossal crash as a set of chandeliers smashed onto the table from above. Great piles of food, including coal-dust-flavoured quail and soot-blackened lobster were catapulted into the air and splattered all over the tapestry-covered walls.

A man's head poked out of a hatch in the roof. "Oops, butterfingers!"

"That's my good but slightly clumsy friend, Harek," interrupted Thorfinn. "Perhaps not the best person to be in charge of lighting."

There were tears in the king's eyes now. "My feast is ruined!" He turned to the ambassador and tried to explain in his best French. "Er, *moi*, er, *verray sorray*!"

The ambassador barked and waved his finger at the king, before storming out.

King Appin's shoulders slumped. "At least none of the other guests are here yet to witness this disaster." Then he checked himself. "Wait, where are my other guests?"

At the king's cue, an attendant threw open the main door at then end of the great hall. Outside it, Olaf was nursing his knuckles, standing on top of a mound of very well-dressed but also very unconscious nobles.

"You told me to get rough with anyone who tried to get in," said Olaf.

"NO!" cried the king. "NO! **NO! NO! NO!** I said anyone *without an invitation*, not just *anyone*."

"Oh, right, sorry." Olaf shrugged.

The king sank to his knees and wept in despair. "Whit is *wrong* with you people? How could this happen to *me?*"

Thorfinn placed a hand on the king's shoulder. This time King Appin couldn't even be bothered to shout at him.

"There, there, your majesty," he soothed. "It's not all bad. I mean, look..." Thorfinn pointed out the figure struggling up the stairs towards them, breathing heavily and dragging a box behind him. It was Torsten, back from the cobbler's at last.

"Here's your shoes, your highness!" he declared.

King Appin shook Thorfinn off and got to his feet, yelling, "You're all fired, the lot of you! Now GET OUT!!!"

CHAPTER 13

The following day, on the outskirts of Dunadd City, Thorfinn and his friends sat round a table in the tumbledown wooden shack they now called home.

"It's not much fun being unemployed, is it?" said Torsten, slumped with his head in his hands.

"Pity. Food-tasting was the best job I ever had," said Grut wistfully.

"It's the only job you've ever had," said Olaf.

"I loves'd them castle kitchens," said Gertrude. "They hads a lovely supply of juicy slugs."

During their brief stay at King Appin's castle,

Thorfinn had set the crew to work scouring every corner for the treasure, but they had found nothing. Velda had been planning to hide in chimneys and eavesdrop, and Thorfinn had been intending to listen in at discussions during the feast. But, of course, thanks to Olaf, no guests had made it to the feast. And there was still no sign of the missing galley.

Finding new jobs was proving difficult. Mr Wibblish had finally realised that his Viking Job Centre had been a complete waste of time because Vikings were totally and utterly unemployable.

"No one wants to touch us with a longship oar," whined Oswald.

"Can't we just go home?" suggested Torsten.

Thorfinn stood up. "My dear friends, we might

have run out of leads for finding the treasure, but there's still time – we have a few days before we need to set sail for Indgar. We must stay positive and watchful – and most importantly we need to eat to stay strong and healthy!"

"So what should we do?" they asked.

"Why, we'll bake scones," he replied. "Baking always makes me feel better." And so, they set about building a fire and baking some scones. They soon ate them, and as they still had nothing to do, they baked some more.

"Hmmm," said Velda, biting into her sixth scone. "Why don't we try and sell these scones?"

They set up a makeshift market stall in the streets. When they'd sold out, they baked even more scones. Loads and loads of them. They sold so many they had to move into a disused baker's shop, where they baked hundreds and hundreds of scones. They hung a sign over the door that read:

THORFINN INC.
NICEST SCONEMAKERS

"Right! I'm in charge of this operation," said Velda, staring out at everyone from under the rim of her helmet, "so I need a job title. I'll be the CSO – Chief Scone Officer."

"Oh, goodie, can we all have job titles?" asked Thorfinn.

Grut was first to thrust his arm in the air.

"Ooh, ooh, ooh! Can I be 'Scone Salesman'?"

"Salesman? Ha!" yelled Olaf. "You're rubbish at sales – you just pretend you've sold them and then eat them all yourself!"

Thorfinn decided they would draw lots to decide their job titles.

Harek went first, yanking a piece of parchment out of Thorfinn's helmet. He stared down at it blankly. "I can't read."

Thorfinn took it for him and read it out: "Harek, congratulations, you are now our Health and Safety Officer."

Everyone burst out laughing, except Harek, who fumed. "What are you laughing at?" He tripped over a sack of flour and collapsed spreadeagled on the floor.

Oswald drew the next piece of parchment
from the hat. "I'm our Office Manager, in charge of
paperwork. Oh, good, that means I can have a nice
sit down."

Next was Grimm, who warily handed his piece of
parchment to Thorfinn.

"My dear friend," said Thorfinn, "you're our Events Manager, in charge of organising our staff night out."

"Oh," said Grimm sadly. "There's an undertaker along the street. Maybe we could hold the staff party there?"

Then came Torsten. "You're our Delivery Man," said Thorfinn.

"You must be joking! He couldn't deliver an envelope, never mind a batch of scones," said Olaf.

Thorfinn himself drew Head Chef, along with Gertrude the Sous Chef and Grut the Pot Washer. Thorfinn's main task was trying to stop Grut from eating the scones.

"Oh, can't I just taste another one?" asked Grut,

making a sign with his thumb and forefinger. "Just a leetle one?"

"How abouts a beetle one?" Gertrude offered, which soon shut him up.

Sales went through the roof, although that might have been down to Velda's selling technique. She stood in the marketplace, a tray of scones hanging round her neck. "Oi! Grandad!" she cried at one passing old man. "I said buy my scones – or else!"

"But I've got nae teeth!" replied the man.

"So?!" she replied, thrusting two scones into his hand. "You can suck on 'em!"

That afternoon, Velda sat in their office with her feet on the desk, counting pennies. "We're making money," she said, "but we'll never have enough to pay back Magnus the Bone-Breaker! We need to find that treasure."

At that moment Harek burst through the door, breathless. "Velda, come quickly! You must see this."

She leapt to her feet. "What is it?"

"A massive boat with forty oars just arrived in the harbour."

CHAPTER 14

Velda grabbed Thorfinn, who
was covered in flour, and
Olaf, who was skulking
around outside the back
door looking for someone to
beat up.

They followed Harek down to
the harbour, where they hid behind some barrels
and peered at the ships.

"There, see!" Harek pointed out a galley just a
hundred metres away.

"That's definitely the same boat," said Olaf.

A horse-drawn wagon stood on a jetty alongside the ship. It was carrying a heavy load hidden under a large black cover.

"And I bet that's our treasure," said Velda.

Armed men wearing hooded cloaks were stepping off the boat. They looked around suspiciously, as if ready for trouble at any moment.

A tall figure with ginger hair poking out from under his hood caught Velda's attention. "Wait, wait..." She slapped herself on the forehead as she realised. "That's it! Now I know how they did it. Back on the treasure island when you were guarding the chest, one of those hooded guys barged into me as I was carrying your food. He must have slipped something into your drinks!"

"I knew it," said Olaf.

Another figure strutted down the gangplank. It was Magnus the Bone-Breaker, and he was beaming from ear to ear.

"Bone-Breaker!" breathed Olaf. "He was behind this the whole time."

"That explains why the galley took so long to reach Dunadd," said Thorfinn. "They must have hidden in a loch, waiting for Magnus to circle back south and catch up."

One of the hooded men took the horses' reins and the wagon rolled forward. More guards pushed and jostled their way through the crowds, shouting, "Move it! Clear a path in the name of the king!"

Velda punched her palm. "They're heading to the castle! So here's the plan..." The others crouched closer, listening. "Me and Thorfinn will follow the wagon. Harek, you and Olaf go and fetch the others.

Meet us at the castle."

Olaf and Harek darted off up a side street, while Velda and Thorfinn joined the crowd that had gathered to watch the wagon. The ship's arrival had caused a stir of excitement in the town. The streets were bustling and people were leaning out of their windows to get a good view.

The wagon halted in the square outside the castle entrance. Velda and Thorfinn crouched behind a wall and watched.

King Appin was standing on a platform wearing a golden crown. He greeted Magnus the Bone-Breaker like an old friend.

Then the armed guards threw off their hooded cloaks to reveal themselves. They were all Scottish warriors wearing red-and-blue tartan. The tall warrior with the ginger beard hauled the black cover off and sure enough, there was the treasure chest!

Thorfinn and Velda couldn't hear what Magnus and the king were saying, but Magnus suddenly threw his arm out in a wide gesture towards the treasure. The king replied by throwing his own arm out towards a group of fierce soldiers standing nearby, all wearing chainmail and armour and carrying battle shields.

"I wonder what they're up to?" said Thorfinn.

"Magnus is buying gallowglasses from the king,"
came Oswald's whiny voice from behind them.
He had arrived with the rest of the crew.

"What are gallowglasses?" asked Velda.

"Paid soldiers. Elite warriors from the outer islands."

"Pah!" she said. "There aren't many of them.
What can he do with so few men?"

"They're just the commanders," said Oswald.

117

"There will be more. For that amount of treasure he could buy a whole army."

"Oh dear," said Thorfinn. "With his own army, I fear Mr Bone-Breaker could take over all of Norway."

Velda gasped. "He could defeat the royal army, and claim the throne of Norway."

Magnus and the king turned and walked side by side into the castle, followed by the guards and the wagon.

"We have to stop him," said Olaf. "But how?"

Thorfinn grinned. "Don't worry, everyone. I have a plan."

CHAPTER 15

A short while later, Thorfinn and his crew took deep breaths and stepped into the square in front of the castle. They were dressed up in pink sheets that had been raided from a washing line and cut roughly to look like dresses. They were adorned with ribbons and buttons, and even, in Gertrude's case, a bell and collar she'd nicked from round a cat's neck.

"My dear friends," said Thorfinn, "please allow me to do the talking. And do try to be as womanly as possible. That is, if it's not too inconvenient."

Grut answered in a posh, high-pitched voice, "YE-AS Thorfinn!"

Olaf mumbled under his breath and shook his head. "This is *not* how Vikings should look."

At the gate, they crowded round the tall ginger-bearded guard, doing a shimmying, swaying kind of dance, just like Oswald had told them to.

The guard pushed him away, sneering. "Get off! Who are you?"

"We," said Thorfinn, "are the Fair Maids of Mull. We're performers for the feast this evening."

The guard eyed the knobbly knees poking out from under their dresses. "Oh, ye are, are ye? Go on then, give us a tune."

The crew glanced at each other, then Thorfinn

broke into song. He had a fine, high singing voice.

"There was a young maiden from bonnie Dundee... Tra-la-la-la—"

"OUCH!" yelled Grut, jumping into the air and interrupting the song. "Who touched my bum?" He coughed then switched to his high-pitched voice. "Who did it? Was it you?" He glowered at Torsten, who was right beside him.

Gertrude giggled, chewing. "No, it was me, there was a fly on it."

"You dare accuse me of touching your rotten old bum?!" replied Torsten in a similar high-pitched voice. The two men started slapping each other, while the others frantically tried to stop them.

For a split second, Thorfinn's cunning plan threatened to go disastrously wrong – until the guards burst out laughing.

"Ah, we get it! You're obviously the comedy act. " The ginger-haired guard stood aside, chuckling to himself, and waved them on. "In you go."

The staff were all so busy preparing for the feast that no one inside the castle paid them any attention.

Oswald dangled a small bottle from his finger. "I pickpocketed that guard. I think you'll find it's the same potion he used on you. Leave it with me and Gertrude," said Oswald, turning towards the kitchens. "A few drops in the mead should do the trick."

Giant platters of food were being carried in the direction of the great hall.

"That-a-way!" said Thorfinn, and he led the others along another passageway, past stewards, jugglers and servants. They stopped outside a set of double doors and Thorfinn peeked through the crack. "Ah-ha!" he said. "I see it!"

The treasure chest sat proudly in the centre of the hall, lying open to display the jewels within.

Long tables were set up around the chest, lined with many nobles, some of whom were still nursing black eyes, thanks to Olaf. At the head table, on a raised platform, sat King Appin and Magnus the Bone-Breaker.

"What's happening?" asked Velda.

"Good news," said Thorfinn, spying some servants who were bringing large jugs from the kitchens. "The mead is being brought in. I hope Gertrude and Oswald managed to tip in the potion."

Just as the servants were pouring the mead, the double doors in front of Thorfinn and his crew were flung open and they were pushed into the hall and onto the stage. A courtier announced, "Please welcome... the Fair Maids of Mull!"

Polite applause gave way to bemused silence, before Thorfinn and his crew realised that all eyes were on them and their hairy legs.

CHAPTER 16

"Oh dear," said Thorfinn.

"What do we do now?" whispered Velda through her teeth.

Thorfinn took a deep breath, stepped forward, bowed and took the hands of Grut and Velda.

"Follow me, everyone," he said.

The other Vikings followed his lead, clasping each other's hands. Thorfinn began moving backwards and forwards, swinging his legs, and they copied him. This went on for a moment in deathly silence.

"Vikings *do not* dance," Olaf grumbled under his breath.

Harek started humming an old Viking tune, the title of which roughly translated as: 'Chuck the bishop in the sea and pelt him with cabbages'.

"Yo-yo, yo, yo, yo, yo-yo, yo, yo, yo!" Harek sang, nodding and straining to smile.

"Yo-yo, yo, yo, yo, yo-yo, yo, yo, yo!" they all

repeated, their smiles straining even more.

King Appin rose to his feet. His face was trembling with anger and his eyes were wide with recognition. "You lot – again!"

But all of a sudden the king's eyes drooped. He slumped forward, landing with a huge SPLAT in a giant jelly.

Only then did Thorfinn notice that everybody else in the hall, including Magnus, was face down in their dinner too.

At that moment Oswald and Gertrude burst in. "The guards are also asleep," Oswald announced.

"Yes, tee-hee," giggled Gertrude. "We gave them all a leetle drinkie."

"Well done, everyone," said Thorfinn. "But there's no time to lose. Magnus will wake up soon, and his boat is faster than the *Green Dragon*."

Velda threw off her pink sheet and rolled up her sleeves. "Right, you pig-dogs, let's get this treasure back to Indgar! We only have a few days, and a long voyage ahead!"

CHAPTER 17

Several days later, back in Indgar, Magnus the Bone-Breaker strutted down the main street, halting every once in a while to gawp and laugh at the terrified villagers. "Ha! Who put your face on the wrong way round? Look at these poor wretches!"

He arrived at the marketplace to find Harald the Skull-Splitter sitting hunched and forlorn over a desperately small mound of gold and jewellery. Erik the Ear-Masher was slumped on a low wall nearby, his head in his hands. Thorfinn's mother, Freya, stood looking down her nose at them both.

"Is this all you managed to scrape together?" asked Magnus. "It's pathetic!"

"Shut it, Bone-Breaker!" barked Harald.

"Can't you give us some more time?" pleaded Erik. "Just a few days."

"No chance," barked Magnus. "Your fourteen days

are up. You know what that means. Hand over the keys to your cowshed."

Harald sighed a long deep sigh of surrender. "There is nothing else we can do."

Magnus stood in front of them, his hands on his hips, gloating. "I might have lost the treasure, but this is worth it. At long last Indgar will be mine, and I won't have to live next door to you fools any longer. If only that silly son of yours and his daft bird could see your faces right now – then it would be perfect."

At that moment he was startled by a flap of wings beside his ear.

It was a pigeon.

Thorfinn's pigeon, Percy.

And it landed on his head and craned its neck to look down at his face.

"What in the name of Odin's trousers...?!"

Magnus turned to see the crew of the *Green Dragon*, led by none other than Thorfinn, pulling a wagon into the marketplace. Nobody, it seemed, had noticed their ship slipping into the fjord and mooring at the pier.

Thorfinn removed his helmet and saluted. "Good day, dear Father and Mother. How pleased I am to see you again." His mum Freya rushed over to hug him.

"Thorfinn?!" bellowed Harald. "My boy!"

"What would you like us to do with this?" Velda asked as Torsten and Harek leaped onto the wagon,

threw off the cover and prised open the lid of the treasure chest.

Gold once again glittered in Chief Harald the Skull-Splitter's eyes, while fear shone in those of Magnus the Bone-Breaker.

"But how...?" spluttered Magnus. "They told me it had been stolen by *dancing ladies*! I thought those

Scots had tricked me—"

"Chief Harald," Velda cut in. "Magnus tricked us all and stole the treasure. He wanted to buy an army from King Appin of Scotland."

"WHATT!?" roared Harald. He leapt to his feet. His eye twitched furiously at Magnus. "You filthy dog!"

Magnus's eyes glazed over with terror. "Oh, er, right, er... Oh, dear Thor!" He turned and fled, sprinting out of the village.

The villagers, who had only a few minutes ago been miserable, gave a great cheer and chased after him, pelting him with turnips.

Harald knelt down in front of his son and placed a mighty hand on his shoulder. "Thorfinn,

my dear, dear boy, you've saved us yet again.
I'm so sorry. Why do I ever doubt you?"

"Think nothing of it, dear Father. I'm just glad to
be home." Thorfinn patted his other shoulder and
Percy flapped onto it. "Come on, old bean, let's go
for a nice cup of tea and a sit down."

With that, Thorfinn trotted off, whistling, leaving
the rest of the Vikings to admire the treasure.

"Ha!" cried Erik. "Can you believe it? We're rich
again! And we get to keep Indgar!"

Velda stifled a laugh. She didn't have the
heart to tell them Thorfinn had already donated
the treasure to a charity, The Mangy Elks Protection
League, who were coming to pick the whole lot up
that afternoon.

RICHARD THE PICTURE-CONQUEROR

DAVID THE STORY-CHIEF

DAVID MACPHAIL left home at eighteen to travel the world and have adventures. After working as a chicken wrangler, a ghost-tour guide and a waiter on a tropical island, he now has the sensible job of writing about yetis and Vikings. At home in Perthshire, Scotland, he exists on a diet of cream buns and zombie movies.

RICHARD MORGAN was born and raised by goblins on the Yorkshire moors. After running away to New Zealand to play with yachts and paint backgrounds for Disney TV he returned to the UK to write and illustrate children's books. He now lives in Cambridge, England, and has a family of goblins of his own.

THORFINN'S TREASURE HUNT

Follow the clues to help Thorfinn find the buried treasure.

1. Your longship has landed on Treasure Island – HUZZAH! Tie your boat up on the beach at C2.

2. Sneak 1 square ⚡ then run 3 squares ⚡ over bumpy ground. Oswald has been doing his washing again!

3. It's a steep climb 1 square ⚡. Watch out for the mangy elk.

4. A quick sprint downhill now, but don't trip on the slippery fish.

5. Head ⚡, but watch out for Gertrude and her beetle scones.

6. Take a stroll ⚡ along the beach, past the hungry sea monster then 2 squares ⚡. Whoa, there's a pooey smell!

7. You're nearly there! Go ⚡ 2 squares, dodging past Harald's axes.

8. Have you found the treasure? Write the grid reference here ___ ___ and check on page 144.

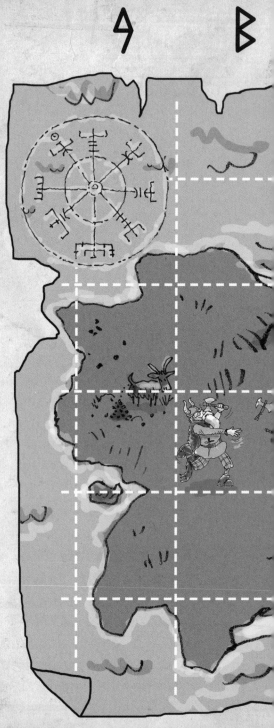

VIKING JOB CENTRE

(not so) promising candidates

NAME: Percy

CURRENT JOB: Pigeon

PLACE OF BIRTH: The big hedge behind the blacksmith's, Indgar village, Norway.

EDUCATION: Old Bess's school of pigeonry.

SKILLS: Stealing Thorfinn's scones (without him knowing).

NAME: Velda

CURRENT JOB: Ferocious Viking warrior, RAAAR!

PLACE OF BIRTH: Grrrr! What's with all the questions?

EDUCATION: Entire days wasted listening to Oswald prattle on about geography.

SKILLS: Axe-throwing, brawling, bashing. Can catapult myself over castle walls. I'm a good aim with a fish.

NAME: Oswald

CURRENT JOB: Wise man of Indgar village.

PLACE OF BIRTH: I don't remember, I was just a baby.

EDUCATION: Diploma in Wisdom from Mad Meg the Wandering Druid of Oslo.

SKILLS: Burping champion (retired), translator (retired), teacher. Can do high kicks and sleep standing up... ZZZZZZZZ.

Answer: square C4